This book belongs to

....

and their

SUPERHERO DAD

MY DAD IS A SUPERHERO

Written by **Ruby Brown**

Illustrated by **Lesley Vamos**

Sandy Creek
NEW YORK

My dad is a

He can **FLY** really high.

His **INVISIBILITY POWERS** are awesome.

He can
PREDICT THE FUTURE.

And he is a
SUPER GENIUS.

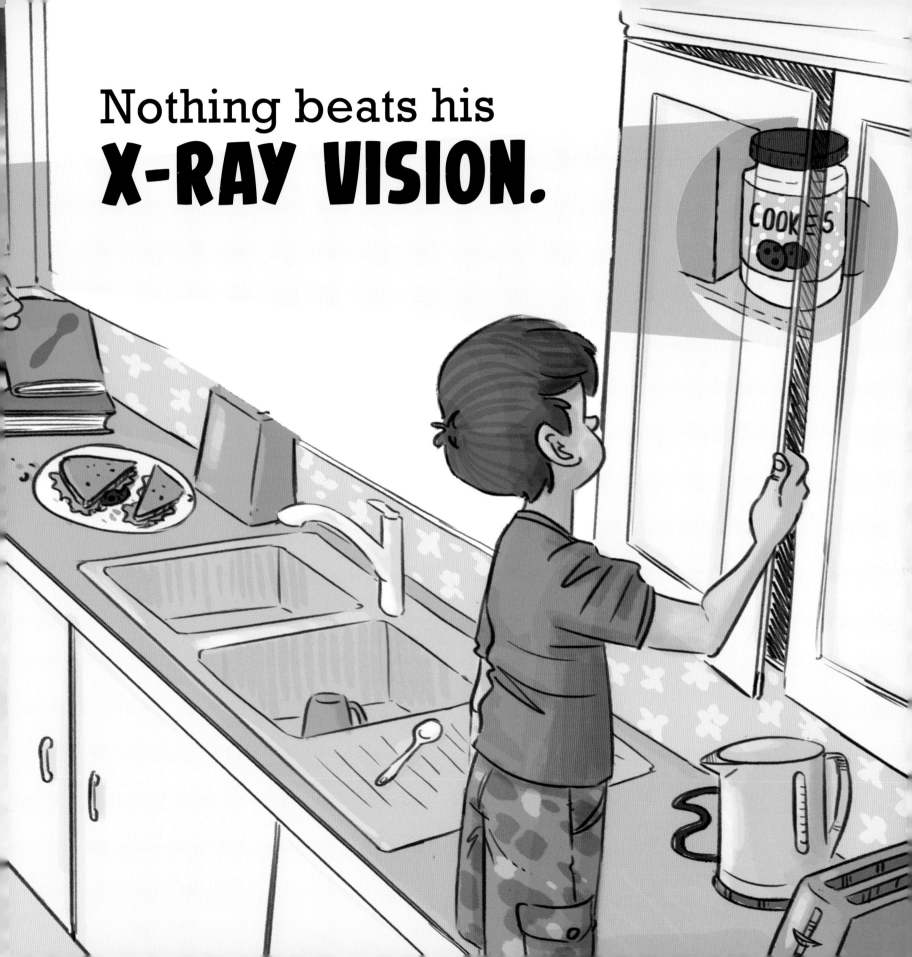

But I wouldn't mind if he lost his
MIND CONTROL POWERS.

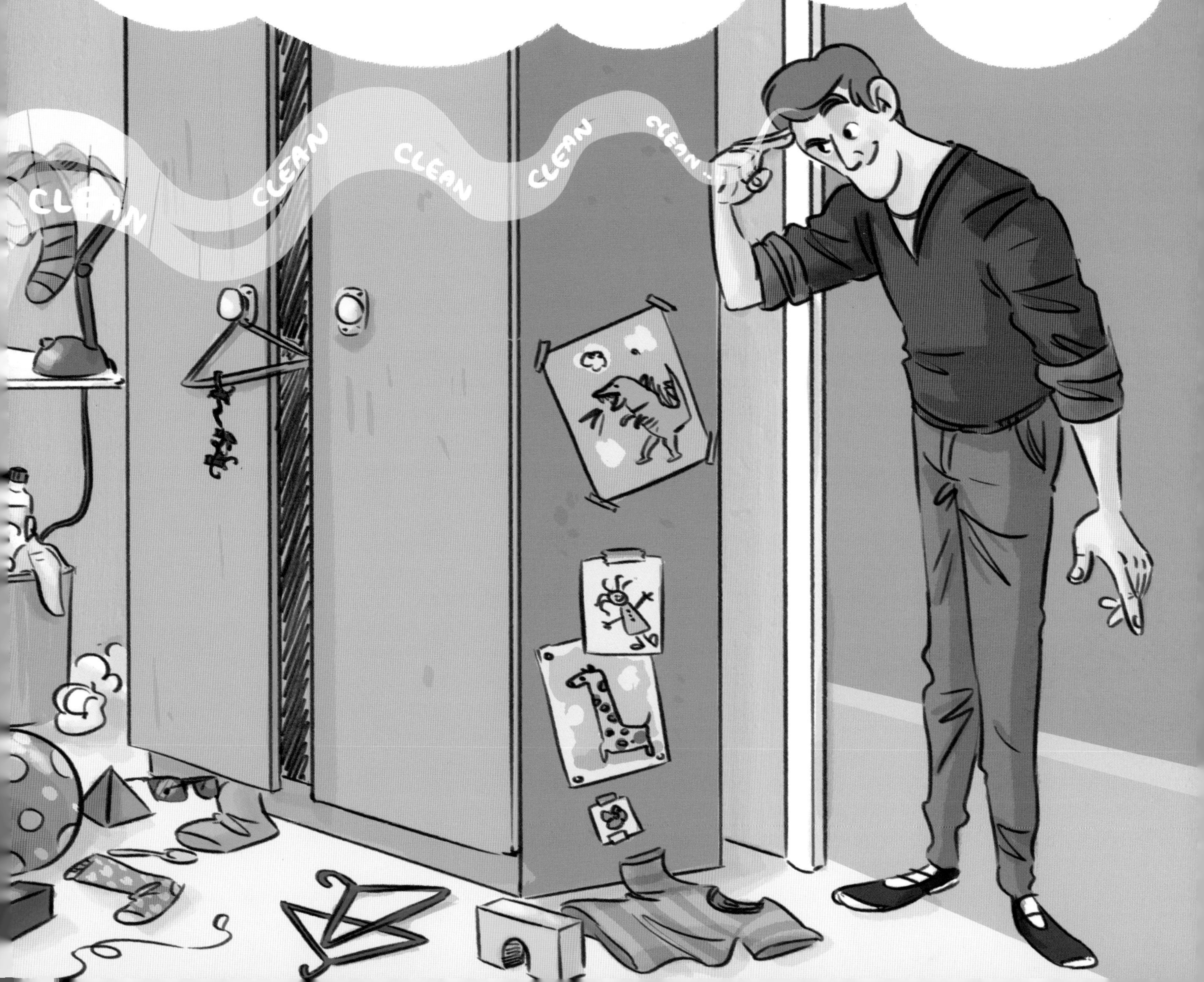

My dad is **MY SUPERHERO.**

An imprint of Sterling Publishing
387 Park Avenue South
New York, NY 10016

SANDY CREEK and the distinctive Sandy Creek logo
are registered trademarks of Barnes & Noble, Inc.

Text, illustration and design copyright © 2013 Hardie Grant Egmont
Illustrations by Lesley Vamos
Design by Ash Oswald @ Hey There's Me

This 2014 edition published by Sandy Creek.

ISBN 978-1-4351-5488-9

Manufactured in Shenzhen, China

Lot #:

2 4 6 8 10 9 7 5 3 1

02/14